SPECTRAL ECHOES

GHOSTLY TALES & HAUNTING VERSES

BY C.M. WYCKOFF

ILLUSTRATIONS BY AARON LINDEMAN

SIXTEEN 37

OMNIMEDIA

Spectral Echoes by C.M. Wyckoff

Copyright ©2025 by Sixteen 37 Omnimedia, ltd

First Printing, 2025.

ISBN: 979-8-9924611-1-4

First Edition: January 2025

Illustrations and Cover Art by Aaron Lindeman

Table of Contents

PREFACE

As a child, Halloween was more than just a night of collecting crazy amounts of candy - it was a portal to a realm of magic and mystery. Each year, as the air grew crisp and leaves began to cover the ground in fiery hues, I eagerly awaited the arrival of All Hallows' Eve. It wasn't just about the candy or the costumes; it was about the thrill of the unknown, the chill that ran down my spine as darkness descended and the world transformed.

My mother would often indulge my passion though she never liked Halloween herself. One year she literally drew a face on a brown paper bag and cut holes out where my eyes would peek through. Another year she bought me what I thought was the coolest costume ever; Batman!

As I grew older, my fascination with Halloween took on a darker hue. It was my sisters who first introduced me to the world of Horror movies-the kind that made your heart race and your skin prickle with anticipation. The kind that would keep me up at night wondering if some knife wielding serial killer was hiding in my closet! We would huddle together in the dim glow of the television, snacks of some sort being strewn across the floor as I watched the terror unfold onscreen.

Amongst the myriad of horror films, one stood out above the rest: the supernatural tale of "The Haunting of Hill House." Shirly Jackson's words leapt off the page and seared themselves into my consciousness, igniting a passion for gothic horror that would shape my literary tastes for years to come. The eerie atmosphere, the subtle whispers of malevolence lurking in the shadows-it was a masterclass in psychological terror that left an indelible mark on my soul.

From that moment on, my fascination with haunted houses, the macabre, and gothic romance deepened. I devoured books that promised to send shivers down my spine, often set in opulent yet decaying Victorian mansions. And as I delved deeper into that realm of horror, I discovered that there was a certain beauty in the darkness, a twisted allure that drew me inexorably closer.

Now, as I sit amidst a pile of dog-eared novels and flickering candles, I realize that my love for Halloween and all things creepy has become more than just a childhood fascination-it's a part of who I am. And as I embark on this journey into the depths, I can't help but feel a thrill of excitement at the thought of what lies ahead.

Take my hand, turn the page, and let's begin…

HAUNTING VERSES

The Ghosts of Memory

In the grand estate, with halls so wide,
A young man roams with quiet pride.
He speaks with cheer, his laughter light,
In the day, and through the night.

"Mother dear, how do you fare?
Father, I see you in your chair.
Sister, brother, gather near,
Let's reminisce on times so dear."

In the Great Hall, with portraits tall,
He finds his kin, one and all.
Their painted eyes, so lifelike, bright,
Fill his days and endless nights.

Yet shadows creep in corners dim,
A truth that stays concealed from him.
For in his mind, they're flesh and bone,
In reality, he's all alone.

The manor groans with age's weight,
Its splendor turned to dismal state.
Cobwebs cling and dust descends,
As time its haunting sorrow sends.

He walks the halls with steadfast gait,
Ignoring whispers of cruel fate.
Locked within his own domain,
Where only memories and ghosts remain.

Old friends arrive, with worry fraught,
To find the one they long had sought.
They search the halls, the rooms so grand,
Till in the Great Hall, they make their stand.

There he sits, in chair so fine,
A smile on lips, in death's recline.
Gazing up with eyes serene,
At portraits of his cherished dream.

"Mother dear, how do you fare?
Father, I see you in your chair.
Sister, brother, gather near,
Let's reminisce on times so dear."

The friends, in silence, understand,
The depth of sorrow that life had planned.
For in his mind, his family stayed,
But in this world, they had decayed.

Locked within his memories' hold,
The young man's tale of sorrow told.
In the decayed estate, so grand and tall,
His spirit lingers in the Great Hall.

THE GHOSTLY FOREST

In shadows deep, where moonlight barely gleams,
There lies a forest where the spirits roam.
Where whispers dance upon the wind's dark seams,
And eerie echoes haunt the ancient loam.

Tall trees stand sentinel in moon's soft glow,
Their branches reach for the starlit sky.
Beneath their canopy, where secrets flow,
The supernatural comes drifting by.

Ghosts of the past, with tales left untold,
Wander through the mist with silent tread.
Their presence felt, though mysteries unfold,
In the tangled roots and paths the living dread.

Glimmering shadows flit through twisted vines,
A ghostly choir hums a mournful tune.
The fog thickens where the moonlight shines,
As restless phantoms waltz beneath the moon.

Ancient oaks shiver with a spectral breath,
Leaves whisper secrets of forgotten lore.
Echoes of love, betrayal, and death
Resound in whispers evermore.

In this enchanted wood, the night holds sway,
Where the supernatural comes to play.
The bravest souls dare not intrude,
For in these woods, the darkness stays.

THE GATES

Beware the gates that stand so tall,
With iron bars and ghostly sprawl.
They're meant to guard what lies within,
A realm of secrets, a world of sin.

These gates, they creak with eerie glee,
A warning whispered through the key.
For what's confined behind those bars,
Is not from Earth, but from the stars.

Beyond those gates, shadows creep,
In the silence, secrets seep.
Darkness dances, tendrils twine,
A realm where nightmares intertwine.

The locks may hold, the chains may bind,
Yet the true horror lies entwined.
For gates, though sturdy, may betray,
What dwells inside, night and day.

Not to keep the living out,
But to trap the whispers, screams, and doubt.
Within those bars, a ghastly sight,
A haunting specter, a moonless night.

Beware the gates, and what they seal,
A malevolent force that's all too real.
For what they hide, you can't outrun,
A darkness that eclipses the sun.

Gates may guard, but some betray,
The terrors locked in the light of day.
Look not just out, but deep within,
For the true horrors that gates begin.

THE LONELY MANSION

In the heart of the woods, where shadows linger,
Stands a mansion, once proud, now a ghostly figure.
Silent halls echo with the weight of time,
A lonely manor, a forlorn rhyme.

Majestic and grand, it looms in despair,
Once filled with laughter, now trapped in the air.
Tapestries of velvet, draped in decay,
Beauty now fading, memories astray.

Portraits of ancestors in ornate frames,
Witness to ages, forgotten names.
Eyes that once sparkled, now vacant and cold,
Stories of old, their tales left untold.
Dust-covered splendor, a haunting grace,
Chandeliers weep in the empty space.
Whispers of bygone days echo through,
Faint remnants of life, a spectral clue.

Cobwebs cling to the grand staircase,
A silent witness to the grandeur's disgrace.
Loneliness shrouds each forgotten room,
In the fading twilight's spectral gloom.

Moonlight filters through the tattered lace,
Casting shadows on the once-polished face.
Furniture draped in melancholy veils,
Ghosts of opulence, their beauty pales.

The gardens overgrown, nature reclaimed,
The mansion stands witness to time's cruel game.
A ballroom where waltzes once filled the air,
Now echoes with solitude, a lingering despair.

A pianoforte sits in silence and rust,
Keys once played melodies, now covered in dust.
Lonely corridors, memories confined,
To the haunting stillness of a mansion enshrined.

Yet, in the quiet, a poignant grace,
A spectral beauty in this desolate place.
A melancholy waltz of shadows and light,
In the lonely mansion, lost in the night.

PORTALS OF THE PAST

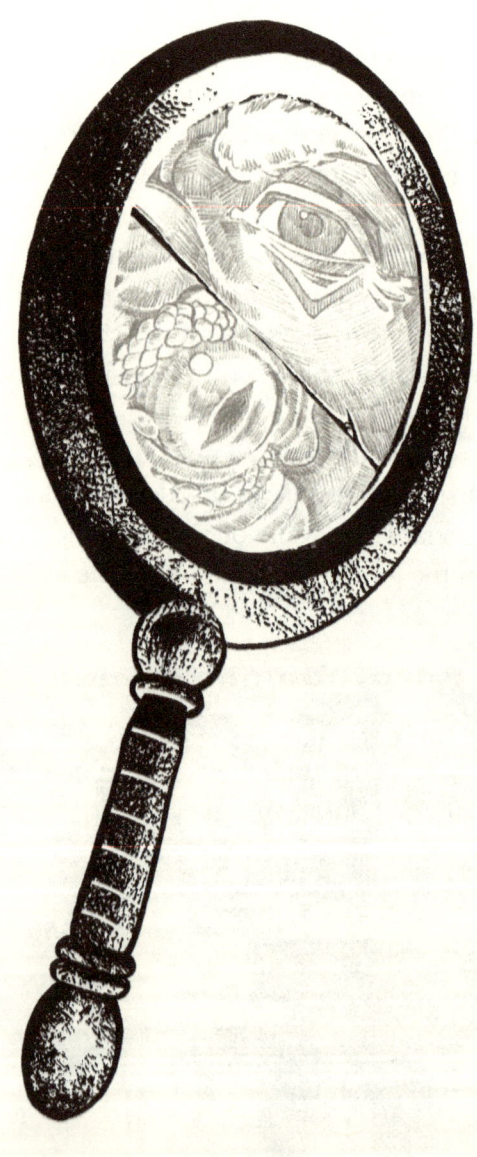

In the silvery glass, reflections gleam,
A mirror's gaze, more than it may seem.
For within its depths, a dark world of dreams,
Where shadows dwell, and ghosts convene.

A portal, thin, yet deep as night,
Through which spirits have mystical sight.
The living see but a fleeting face,
While ghosts peer through, a window space.

In the realm of mirrors, time stands still,
A conduit for the restless to engage at will.
They watch our world with silent eyes,
Traveling through, where the mirror lies.

In the depths of night, when shadows play,
Ghosts slip through, in spectral array.
From time and space, with haunting laugh,
Entering homes, through mirror's, their path.

The glass, a doorway, open wide,
To realms where living and ghostly reside.
A bridge unseen, yet ever near,
Where echoes of the past are sure to appear.

So gaze not long, nor linger there,
For the mirror's depths hold spirits' glare.
They watch, they wait, they traverse the span,
Between the worlds of ghost and man.

THE LADY IN THE MIRROR

In the heart of Ohio stands an old abode,
An historic house where dark tales are told.
We moved within its ancient halls,
Where whispers echoed off the walls.

At first, mere sounds—just running feet,
Low voices murmuring, whispers discreet.
Bangs and crashes in the dead of night,
Yet not a soul appeared in sight.

Worried, we searched for signs of life,
A burglar's trace or animal strife.
But empty rooms and vacant air,
Only deepened our growing despair.

One fateful night, in early dawn's light,
I ventured down the stairs, gripped by fright.
In the hall's mirror, a vision clear,
A woman's form began to appear.

In the dining room, her silhouette,
Moved with grace, a ghostly threat.
"Mother," I called, my voice a plea,
But silence answered, chilling me.

Her form was different, not my kin,
A spectral presence lurking within.
Into the kitchen, I quickly sped,
But found no trace, just a creeping dread.

The Lady in the Mirror haunts our days,
With raps on doors, a spectral craze.
Three knocks resound through empty air,
A ghostly rhythm, a phantom's lair.

Her visage clear, pale and stark,
Eyes like voids in the mirror's dark.
She moves with an eerie, silent grace,
A haunting figure, an ageless face.

Cold spots linger where she once tread,
In the kitchen, the maid's quarters, the dread.
In the drawing room, shadows play,
Dancing figures that swiftly sway.

She's a silent watcher in our home,
In the mirror's depths, she's free to roam.
A haunting presence, a chilling plight,
The Lady in the Mirror, veiled in night.

Her story etched in time's embrace,
A spectral mystery, devoid of grace.
In this old house, she will remain,
An eternal watcher, a ghostly bane.

PORTRAIT OF A MAIDEN

In an old and dusty attic, forgotten by the years,
Lies a painting draped in sorrow, soaked with bitter tears.
Its frame is wrought with silver, tarnished, dark, and cold,
Its canvas holds a secret, a story to be told.

The portrait of a maiden, with eyes of deepest black,
A smile that whispers darkness, a gaze that pulls you back.
Her beauty is bewitching, her presence cold as ice,
But beneath her painted surface, lies a twisted vice.

Those who dare a glimpse, feel a shiver down their spine,
A sense of lurking danger, a chill that seems malign.
For the maiden in the painting was once of flesh and bone,
A sorceress of shadows, who feared to die alone.

She poured her soul into the art, her essence trapped inside,
Cursed to haunt the canvas, forever she would bide.
Her eyes would follow movements, her smile would slowly fade,
Drawing those who viewed her into the curse she had made.

The first was a collector, who found her in a sale,
He hung her in his parlor, where guests began to pale.
They heard her whispered secrets, felt her icy breath,
One by one they vanished, claimed by the maiden's death.

A family moved in next, unaware of what they'd found,
They placed her in the hallway, where footsteps made no sound.
The children woke with nightmares, the parents filled with dread,
Till all that filled the house were the voices of the dead.

Now the painting lies abandoned, hidden from the light,
Awaiting the next victim to wander into sight.
So if you find a portrait, of a maiden cold and fair,
Beware the cursed painting, and the doom that lingers there.

For her eyes still seek the living, her smile hides her hate,
And those who fall beneath her spell will share her cursed fate.
An endless sleep of darkness, a life within the frame,
Forever bound to torment, by the maiden with no name.

HALLOWEEN NIGHT

Beneath the crescent moon's pale glow,
On Halloween night, when shadows grow.
A chilling wind whispers through the trees,
A symphony of spooks carried on the breeze.
Jack-o'-lanterns flicker with an eerie light,
Casting shadows that dance in the night.
In the graveyard, tombstones stand tall,
Echoing secrets, a spectral call.

Witches stir cauldrons with potions amiss,
Bubbling brews in the moonlit abyss.
Black cats slink with eyes ablaze,
As ghosts and goblins join the maze.

Children don costumes of ghoulish delight,
Roaming the streets in the dimming light.
Trick-or-treat echoes in the haunted air,
As ghouls and phantoms begin to stare.

Haunted houses with creaking doors,
Reveal the horrors that darkness stores.
A night where fear and excitement collide,
On Halloween night, when the spirits bide.

The moon casts shadows on the old, gnarled trees,
Whispering secrets carried on the breeze.
In the eerie silence, the unknown takes flight,
On Halloween night, a haunting delight.

THE GIRL WITHOUT A FACE

In the dead of night, when the world is still,
There lurks a presence, an ominous chill.
A little girl without a face,
Hiding in shadows, her secret place.

She emerges from darkness, silent, unseen,
A specter of terror, where nightmares convene.
No eyes to see, no mouth to speak,
Yet she roams the halls, eerie and bleak.

At the stroke of midnight, she comes alive,
Her form is horrifying, no face to derive.
She slinks through the corridors, silent as death,
A phantom child with bated breath.

Into the walls, she disappears,
A whisper in the night, fuel for your fears.
She hides in the shadows, her presence unknown,
Spying through cracks, her chilling throne.

Her presence lingers, an otherworldly wraith,
A haunting reminder of life's shadowed faith.
Beware the girl without a face,
For in the night, she stalks with haunting grace.

She watches and waits, her presence unfound,
A ghostly figure, forever unbound.
In the walls she dwells, a silent spy,
A ghastly presence, lurking nigh.

So when the clock strikes twelve, beware,
For the girl without a face will soon be there.
Hiding in the walls, her secrets kept,
A terrifying reminder of the fear she's crept.

In the dead of night, she'll roam your halls,
A ghostly presence, where darkness falls.
A little girl without a face to trace,
Forever watching, in her hiding place.

The Lady In The Lake

In the stillness of the night, when the moon is high,
A whispering wail echoes, a haunting lullaby.
By the edge of Darkmoor, where shadows quake,
Lives a ghostly siren, the Lady in the Lake.

Her voice is soft, her melody sweet,
Drawing the weary with a beguiling beat.
Hikers and campers, with hearts so bold,
Are enchanted by stories of her treasures untold.

They follow her song through the mist and the trees,
Pulled by an urge they cannot appease.
The water's edge glistens, a silvery sheen,
Reflecting the sorrow of a beauty unseen.

With eyes like deep pools, dark and forlorn,
She beckons them closer, to where dreams are torn.
Her arms rise gently, outstretched and pale,
Promising solace in her watery veil.

One by one, they step into the chill,
Hearts captivated, losing their will.
The Lady smiles, her teeth gleaming white,
As they sink beneath, swallowed by the night.

No screams are heard, just the silent, still waves,
Marking the spots of their watery graves.
Their bodies are lost, but their essence she does take,
Feeding the hunger of the Lady in the Lake.

Beware the woods when the moon is high,
And resist the call of her haunting lullaby.
For the Lady in the Lake, with her siren song,
Waits in the darkness, where the lost belong.

THE TOMB

In the heart of night, when the moon's pale gleam,
Casts shadows long, in a macabre dream.
There lies a tomb, where marble coffins sleep,
And restless spirits in darkness creep.

At midnight's hour, the air grows cold,
As echoes of sorrow begin to unfold.
From the depths of the tomb, a freighting sound,
Cries and wails, in a mournful bound.

Each coffin holds a tale untold,
Of lives extinguished, of dreams turned cold.
Their spirits trapped in the cold embrace,
Yearning for release, from this eerie place.

"Join us," they cry, in voices hollow,
Their plea echoes, in the darkness that follows.
Beguiling whispers, a sinister call,
Drawing the living, to their thrall.

But beware, those who dare draw near,
For the tomb holds secrets, dark and drear.
In marble coffins, the dead lay still,
Yet their cries echo, with a chilling shrill.

So heed the warning, and shun their call,
Lest you join the spirits in their haunting hall.
For in the tomb where darkness reigns,
The cries of the dead echo in eternal chains.

THE CURSED URN

In a hidden corner of an antique store,
Lies a vessel of darkness, cursed to the core.
Forgotten by time, whispered tales untold,
A funeral urn, its secrets unfold.

A mortal, with folly, took it home one day,
Unaware of the horrors that within it lay.
Curiosity stirred, they dared to unseal,
The urn's ancient lock, their fate to reveal.

As lid gave way to the darkness inside,
A shiver ran down their spine, they tried
To grasp the enormity of their mistake,
But too late, the curse began to wake.

From depths of shadows, a sinister wail,
Echoed through the halls, a mournful tale.
Spectral hands emerged, reaching out,
To claim the souls of those who dared to doubt.

The air grew thick with a suffocating dread,
As the curse consumed the living and the dead.
Each member of the family met their doom,
In the grip of madness, in the grip of gloom.

Their screams pierced the night, a symphony of despair,
As the urn's dark power devoured with care.
No mercy, no escape, just endless fright,
A macabre dance in the pale moonlight.

And when the last breath had been drawn,
And the cursed urn claimed its final pawn,
Silence fell like a shroud, heavy and cold,
Leaving naught but a tale of horror untold.

Hear this warning, ye who seek,
Beware the urn, its curse so bleak.
For once unleashed, its grip won't wane,
And only darkness shall remain.

DARKNESS, THE END

In the silence of the night, whispers fade,
Echoes of life, in shadows cascade.
For in the end, where all roads bend,
Lies the truth, where none can defend.

Death, the solemn finale, draws its breath,
A journey's end, the quiet of death.
Into the abyss, where no light shines,
Where dreams dissolve, and fate whispers, 'tis time'.

One day the dark will come, unbidden, unwanted,
In its embrace, all sorrows detained.
No flicker of hope, no spark to ignite,
Only the void, in eternal night.

Gone are the colors, the laughter, the pain,
Only the stillness, where nothing remains.
No whispered solace, no tender refrain,
Just the silence of darkness, forever to reign.

So heed the call, for time's relentless train,
And cherish the moments, before they wane.
For in the end, as the shadows reclaim,
One day the dark will come, and in darkness, you'll remain.

THE ETERNAL CYCLE

In the realm where shadows play,
And time's embrace begins to sway,
There stands a gate, both old and wise,
Where earthly bonds meet ghostly ties.

As mortal steps tread paths unknown,
Through fields of dreams and fears we've sown,
They wander lost, in search of light,
Amidst the veil of endless night.

Through whispered winds and silent cries,
They journey on, with weary eyes,
To cross the threshold, leave behind
The world of flesh, the ties that bind.

Yet here, at the gateway's arch,
Where souls converge in solemn march,
They feel the pull of destiny's thread,
As life's curtain draws, the final shred.

And so they pass, from mortal coil,
To realm of spirits, in timeless toil,
Becoming whispers in the breeze,
Ghosts adrift on spectral seas.

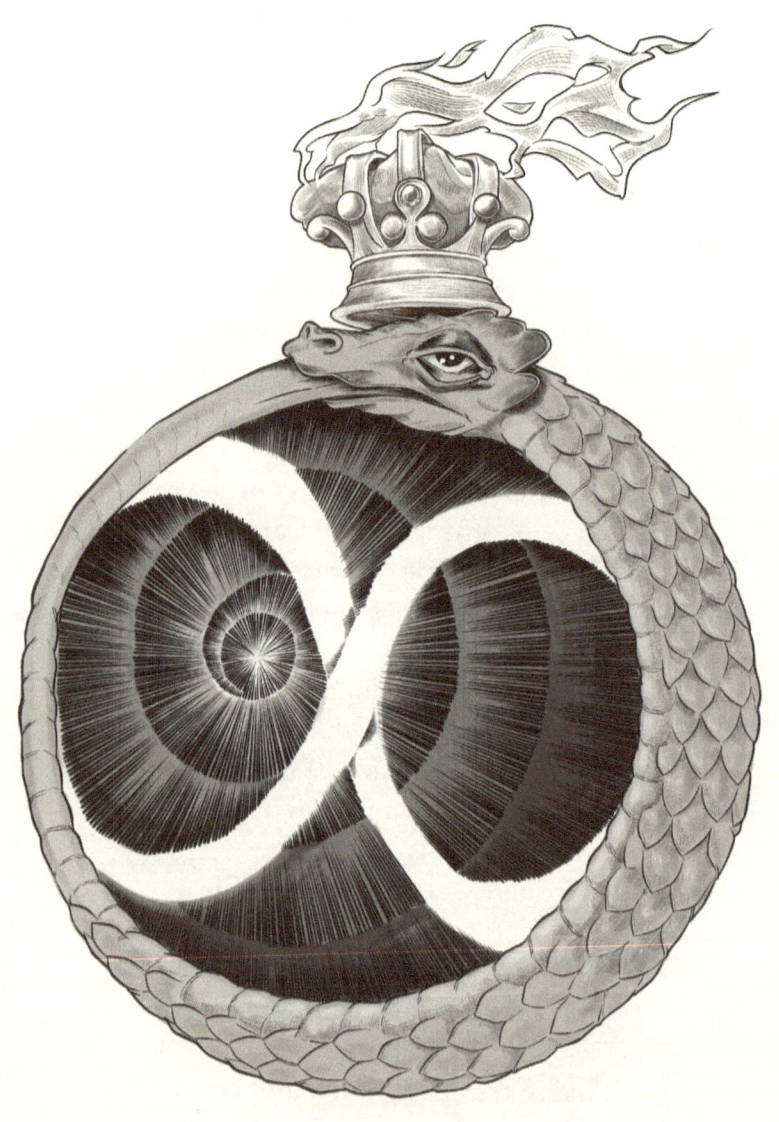

No longer bound by earthly chains,
But lingering still, in spectral pains,
They drift amidst the shadows deep,
Where secrets lie, and memories sleep.

And as they roam the haunted lands,
They find themselves, where it all began,
Before the gates, they stand once more,
But now as ghosts, forevermore.

The journey ends, yet never dies,
For in the echoes of their sighs,
They find the peace they sought in vain,
Amidst the gates, where spirits reign.

So let them wander, lost yet free,
In realms of ghostly mystery,
For here, within the shadows' art,
They find the journey, and the start.

GHOSTLY TALES

Harrowing Hollow

In a small, sleepy town nestled at the edge of a dense forest, there was a place known to the locals as Harrowing Hollow. Rumors abound about that dark and mysterious area, warning of the legend that claimed anyone who ventured into the hollow at night would be lost forever. The stories told of a dark presence that haunted the area, feeding off the fear of those who were foolish enough to wander into the hollow's dark embrace.

Mark, Lisa, Josh, and Emily – longtime friends – scoffed at the legend. They were thrill-seekers, always looking for the next adrenaline rush, and the tales of Harrowing Hollow seemed like the perfect challenge. One autumn afternoon, they resolved to explore the infamous haunted hollow. Arriving as twilight surrendered to darkness, a full moon bathed the landscape in an eerie glow, fueling their determination to debunk the legend.

They grabbed their backpacks and flashlights from the car and, with an unwavering sense of skepticism, made their way to the edge of the

hollow. The entrance was marked by twisted trees and an overgrown path littered with bright yellow and orange leaves, barely visible in the moonlight. Undeterred, the friends ventured in, their laughter echoing through the trees as they joked about the absurdity of the legend and tried to frighten each other by suddenly pointing into the darkness, "What's that?!"

As they walked deeper into the hollow, a chilling silence fell over the forest. The air grew thick with an unnatural fog, and the moonlight struggled to penetrate the dense canopy above. Their joking and laughter ceased as they nervously looked all around them. Mark led the way, using his flashlight to cut through the darkness, but the beam seemed to get swallowed by the shadows.

After what seemed like hours of walking, they reluctantly opted to turn back towards the car. However, as they retraced their steps, they inexplicably found themselves right back at the trailhead, surrounded by the gnarled trees and thick underbrush. Retrieving their phones from their pockets to consult GPS, they discovered their batteries had mysteriously drained. Even their watches had stopped ticking. Perplexed yet resolute, they made another attempt, this time marking their route with stones and snapped branches.

Yet, no matter which direction they took or how many times they tried, they would end up back at the entrance. Panic began to set in as the reality of their situation dawned on them – the legend of Harrowing Hollow was true. They were trapped, and the hollow was feeding off their growing fear.

The friends clung to each other, their nerves beginning to fray as they whispered reassurances that felt increasingly hollow. The oppressive darkness pressed in on them, and the forest seemed to come alive with eerie sounds – whispers, rustling leaves, and distant, otherworldly laughter.

Hours turned into days, though time seemed to lose meaning within the hollow. Exhaustion and terror took their toll, and the friends found it harder to keep their grip on reality. The once-strong bond between them frayed as paranoia set in, each one suspecting the others of causing their dire predicament.

Lisa, her voice trembling, suggested they split up to cover more ground, but the idea was met with vehement opposition. They had seen enough horror movies to know that splitting up would only make things worse. Instead, they huddled together, trying to come up with a plan that would lead them out of the nightmare they had willingly walked into.

But Harrowing Hollow had no intention of letting them escape. The forest seemed to shift around them, its paths changing and twisting, leading them in endless circles. Each attempt to leave was met with the same maddening result – the twisted trees and the overgrown entrance.

As days turned into weeks, their hope dwindled. The hollow fed off their despair, growing stronger as their spirits weakened. One by one, the friends succumbed to the hollow's sinister power. Mark, once the fearless leader, was the first to disappear, swallowed by the darkness. Josh followed, his mind broken by the unrelenting fear. Emily and Lisa clung to each other until the very end, their last moments filled with whispered promises that they would find a way out together. But the hollow had other plans. In the dead of night, Emily vanished, leaving Lisa alone in the suffocating darkness.

With no one left to turn to, Lisa's sanity slipped away, her mind consumed by the hollow's malevolent presence. The legend of Harrowing Hollow had claimed its victims, feeding off their fear until they were no more.

The small, sleepy town continued to tell the story of the Hollow, warning new generations of the fate that awaited those who dared to enter. And the hollow, ever hungry, waited patiently for its next victims, ready to ensnare them in its endless, nightmarish embrace.

The Last Ride

In a desolate corner of America's Midwest, hidden deep within a dense forest, an abandoned amusement park stood as a grim testament to a distant, forgotten past. Once vibrant and bustling with the laughter of children and families, it now loomed ominously among the tall trees and overgrown moss covered pathways, its attractions frozen in time like relics of a haunted carnival. The rusted Ferris wheel groaned mournfully in the wind, its skeletal frame casting long shadows over the overgrown pathways. The carousel, adorned with weathered horses frozen mid-gallop, seemed to watch with hollow eyes as the friends cautiously approached.

The park closed nearly thirty years ago due to severe economic turmoil that struck the town. Most residents left to seek employment and escape the town's decline. However, local legends whispered of a darker fate that befell the park on its grand opening night nearly half a century earlier. Some locals who'd been around for years recounted how the lights had flickered unnaturally, how many of the rides had malfunctioned with deadly consequences, and how the joyful cries of children had turned into agonizing screams. By the morning light, the park lay deserted, its once-cheerful façade marred by tragedy. Years later, a new owner arrived in town with ambitious plans to revive the park, introducing new rides and expanding its attractions to turn a profit. However, fate had other plans. The man, who had no children or family to inherit the park, tragically fell to his death from the

observation tower while taking publicity photos. With no interested buyers and the park's reputation tarnished by the horrific tragedies, it remained closed and never reopened.

What most locals won't tell you—because they don't know, and in fact no one alive knows the true reason—is that the park was built on the site of an old, forgotten cemetery with unmarked graves that had been abandoned more than a century ago. Restless spirits and ancient rites disturbed by the construction began to rise up from their graves. Despite attempts to clear the land and ensure no traces of the cemetery remained, the malevolent energy of the place seemed to seep into the park's foundations.

The years continued to roll by and nature slowly began to consume the park once more. One stormy evening, a group of mischievous friends decided to defy the warnings that echoed through the nearby town. Drawn by the allure of the forbidden and fueled by youthful bravado, they ventured into the depths of the forest, guided only by the distant flashes of lightning and the promise of a macabre thrill.

As they approached the park's rusted gates, warped with age and neglect, a shiver ran down Emily's spine. The heavy iron creaked eerily as if welcoming them into a realm where time held no sway. Against the backdrop of rolling thunder, they hesitated briefly before the gates swung open with a low groan, beckoning them forward into the heart of darkness.

Inside, the air hung heavy with a suffocating silence broken only by the occasional rustle of leaves stirred by a phantom breeze. The smell of rust and dampness wafted through the overgrown terrain. The friends navigated through the labyrinthine pathways, their footsteps echoing hollowly against the cracked pavement. Broken signs swayed ominously overhead, their faded letters spelling out warnings now lost to time. "Let's explore the haunted house," Emily suggested, her voice barely a whisper in the oppressive stillness. With hesitant nods and pounding hearts, they followed her toward the crumbling entrance, its jagged archway resembling the gaping maw of some forgotten beast.

As they crossed the threshold, a chill swept through the air, raising goosebumps on their skin. The darkness within seemed to thicken around them, swallowing their cellphone flashlights' feeble attempts to pierce the gloom. Shadows danced malevolently along the walls, their movements animated by the unseen, while distant whispers slithered through the corridors like serpents of sound.

Deep within the bowels of the haunted house, amidst the debris of shattered illusions and broken dreams, they stumbled upon a decrepit control room. Dust coated every surface, cobwebs hung like veils, and the faint scent of rust mingled with the musty air.

Intrigued and unnerved in equal measure, the friends gathered around the array of old levers and buttons, their curiosity outweighing their growing unease as they brushed the dust and cobwebs away. Emily, the most daring of the group, reached out to grasp a large lever obscured by years of neglect. With a grunt of effort, she attempted to push it upward, only to find it stubbornly resistant to her touch.

Frustration flickered across her face before determination set in. Taking a step back, she drew a deep breath and delivered a powerful kick that sent the lever flying upward with a reverberating clang. Sparks flew from the lever and for a fleeting moment, the distant groan of metal echoed through the house, a sound as eerie as the park itself.

Suddenly, outside in the storm-lashed night, the rides began to stir with a life of their own. The Ferris wheel groaned into motion, its rusted joints protesting against its own gears that began to force motion. The carousel creaked and whirred, its once-merry melody now twisted into a haunting dirge that carried on the wind. And from the depths of the funhouse, shadows began to slither and twist, taking shape in the corners of their vision.

The air grew thick with a discernible sense of dread as they realized too late the gravity of their actions. The park, awakened by their unwitting activation of its dormant machinery, thirsted for retribution. Malevolent whispers swirled around them, their words chilling the very marrow of their bones. "Join us," the voices hissed, their spectral tones mingling with the howling wind. "Don't leave us here alone."

Panic seized the friends as they scrambled to flee, their minds racing with terror-fueled thoughts of escape. But the park had other plans, its old mechanisms creaking into action with a purpose that defied logic or reason. The gates, once swung open in macabre invitation, slammed shut with a finality that echoed like a death knell and thick, thorny vines rapidly began to weave through the iron bars.

Separated by an unseen force, each friend was drawn inexorably toward a different attraction, their fates intertwined with the cursed machinery of the park. Emily found herself ensnared in the relentless grip of the Ferris wheel, its spokes spinning faster and faster until she was a blur of motion and desperate screams. Jack, pursued by ghostly apparitions, stumbled into the carousel's path, its painted horses breaking free from their moorings to circle him with predatory intent.

Sarah and Tom, their hearts pounding in sync with the thunderous beat of the storm, were ensnared within the labyrinthine corridors of the funhouse. Mirrors warped their reflections into grotesque parodies, distorting their features into macabre masks of terror. With every twist and turn, the walls seemed to close in, confounding their attempts to find an escape route that had vanished with the setting sun.

Outside, the storm raged unabated, its fury a mere backdrop to the unfolding nightmare within the park's cursed confines. As the hours wore on and the night deepened, the friends realized with dawning horror the truth that bound them to the cursed park. Their souls, ensnared by the park's insidious grip, were condemned to join the ranks of its spectral inhabitants, forever trapped in a cycle of fear and suffering.

And so, the abandoned amusement park endured as a grim testament to the boundaries between the living and the dead, where the laughter of the past mingled with the cries of the damned. The rides continued their eternal dance, powered by the restless spirits of its victims.

THE CONSERVATORY OF CARNIVOROUS WONDERS

Nestled on the outskirts of a quaint village in England stood the ancient Ashcroft Conservatory, an imposing structure of iron and glass that had been abandoned for decades. Once a marvel of botanical beauty, it now lay in ruins, its glass panels shattered, and its interior overgrown with an impenetrable jungle of vines and foliage. The villagers avoided the conservatory, speaking only in quiet whispers about the strange occurrences that had taken place there.

The Ashcroft Conservatory was built in the late 19th century by Sir Reginald Ashcroft, a renowned botanist with a penchant for collecting exotic and rare plant species. He was particularly fascinated by carnivorous plants and spent years traveling the world to acquire specimens that were both beautiful and deadly. The conservatory became a sanctuary for these unusual plants, which thrived under Sir Reginald's meticulous care.

But as the years went by, strange rumors began to circulate. Villagers

claimed to hear eerie, otherworldly sounds emanating from the conservatory at night—low growls, hissing, and the occasional scream. Then, people started disappearing. It was said that those who ventured too close to the conservatory at night were never seen again. Eventually, the villagers sealed the conservatory and left it to be reclaimed by nature.

In the present day, four siblings—David, Sarah, Mark, and Olivia—had recently inherited the conservatory from a distant relative. Curious and enticed by the potential wealth that the rare plants might bring, they decided to explore the old structure. They collected the keys to the grounds and the conservatory and set out on a misty autumn morning, eager to uncover the secrets of the Ashcroft Conservatory. As they approached the entrance, the air grew thick with the scent of damp earth and decaying leaves. The conservatory loomed before them, its once-grand facade now a skeletal shadow of its former glory. They pushed open the iron doors with a loud, eerie creek and stepped inside, their flashlights cutting through the darkness.

The interior was a tangled maze of overgrown plants and shattered glass. Vines hung from the ceiling like the tendrils of some great beast, and the floor was a carpet of moss and fallen leaves. As they ventured deeper, they began to notice the unusual plants that Sir Reginald had so carefully cultivated. There were pitcher plants the size of barrels, with deep, inviting cavities that seemed to pulse with a faint light. Venus flytraps with jaws as large as dinner plates snapped hungrily at the air, and sundews with glistening tentacles writhed in anticipation.

"These plants are incredible," Mark said, his voice tinged with awe. "We could make a fortune selling them to collectors."

Sarah nodded, but her eyes were wary. "We need to be careful. These plants are dangerous. We should document them first."

They began to explore, taking photos and notes. As they moved through the conservatory, the atmosphere grew increasingly oppressive. The air was thick and humid, and an unsettling silence hung over everything. No sounds from outside the conservatory could penetrate the structure. It was as if the plants were watching them, waiting for the perfect moment to strike.

David was the first to disappear. He had wandered off on his own, fascinated by a particularly large pitcher plant. The others heard his muffled cry for help and rushed to find him, but all that remained were his flashlight and a few drops of blood. Panic set in as they realized the true danger they were in. The conservatory was a deathtrap, and the plants were not merely passive predators. They were intelligent and malevolent, with a hunger for human flesh.

"Stay together!" Olivia shouted, her voice trembling. "We have to get out of here!"

But the conservatory seemed to have other plans. The vines began to move, closing off their exits and herding them deeper into the jungle of deadly flora. Mark was the next to fall, ensnared by a mass of writhing sundew tentacles that pulled him into their sticky embrace. His screams were cut short as the tentacles tightened, suffocating him. The girls watched in horror.

Sarah and Olivia were the only ones left. They stumbled through the foliage, desperately searching for an escape. The plants seemed to grow more aggressive with each passing moment, their movements almost coordinated. Sarah found an old pair of garden shears and picked them up off the floor just as a long vine charged at her. She aggressively snapped the shears closed around the vine and cut it in half, causing it to groan, as if it were human, and forcing it into retreat. Suddenly, a giant Venus flytrap lunged at Olivia, its jaws snapping shut around her torso. Sarah turned to help, but it was too late. She watched in horror as her friend's body was crushed, the sickening sound of bones breaking echoing through the conservatory.

Terrified and alone, Sarah ran, her flashlight flickering in the darkness, the rusty shears in her right hand. She could hear the plants behind her, their leaves rustling and vines slithering. She tripped over a root and fell, her flashlight and the shears skittering away into the shadows. In the dim light, she saw a massive plant looming over her, its gaping maw filled with rows of needle-sharp teeth.

As the plant descended upon her, Sarah's mind flashed back to the warnings of the villagers and the dark history of the Ashcroft Conservatory. Her screams were swallowed by the darkness, and the conservatory fell silent once more.

The Ashcroft Conservatory remains abandoned to this day. Locals continue to avoid it, their memories now filled with the names of the four heirs who had dared to uncover its secrets. The plants within thrived, their hunger sated for now, but always waiting for the next unsuspecting soul to wander into their deadly embrace.

THE SECRET LIBRARY

Deep in the belly of an ancient forest, where the trees whispered secrets to one another as the wind weaved through their branches and mist clung like a shroud, there lay a hidden library, untouched by time. Its existence was known only to a few who had lived to tell their story. Legends and gossip circulated among the locals, who were reluctant to venture too deep into the forest, especially after dark.

Tales spoke of the library's origins, rooted in the dawn of civilization itself, its walls holding the weight of forgotten knowledge and forbidden magic. It was said that the library was older than Eden itself; hidden away after the fall of man and guarded by ancient spirits, bound to its halls by an oath sworn in blood.

One fateful night, under the light of a waning moon, a traveler named Eren stumbled upon the forest's edge. Drawn by curiosity and a thirst for knowledge, he ventured deeper into the mist-shrouded woods until he came upon the library's ivy-covered gates.

As Eren pushed through the gates and stepped through the threshold, he felt a chill run down his spine, as if the very air itself stood perfectly still and whispered warnings of the dangers that lay beyond. Ignoring the ominous sensation, he pressed on, his lantern casting flickering shadows on the ancient tomes that lined the shelves.

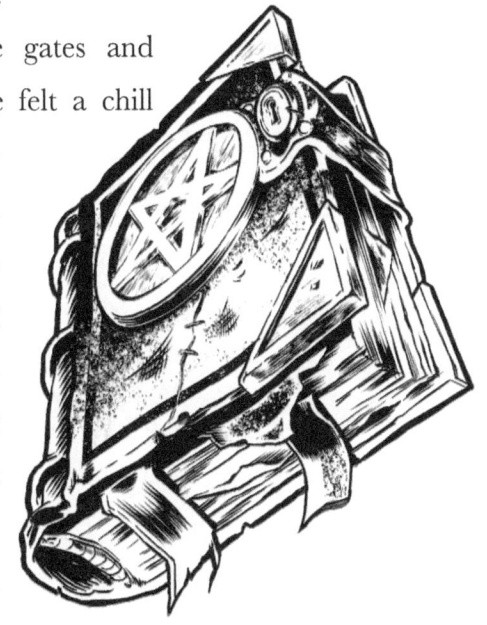

The library seemed to stretch on endlessly, its corridors twisting and turning like a maze of forgotten dreams. Eren's heart raced as he pored over the dusty volumes, each one filled with cryptic symbols and arcane diagrams.

But as the hours passed, he felt a creeping sense of unease settle over him, as if the very walls of the library were alive with malevolent intent. Shadows danced in the corners of his vision, and whispers echoed through the halls, promising secrets too terrible to imagine.

Driven by a desperate thirst for knowledge, Eren tried to ignore the voices in his head and delved deeper into the library's depths, heedless of the dangers that lurked in the shadows. But with each step he took, the darkness seemed to grow stronger, its tendrils wrapping around his mind like chains of iron.

And then, in the darkest corner of the library, Eren stumbled upon a tome unlike any he had ever seen before. Its cover was bound in black leather, its pages etched with runes of unspeakable power.

With trembling hands, he opened the book and began to read, his eyes widening in horror as he uncovered the secrets that lay within. But it was too late—the darkness had already claimed him, its tendrils wrapping around his soul with a grip that could never be broken.

And so, as the mist closed in around him and the whispers of the library's ghosts grew louder, Eren made his choice. He would become one with the darkness, his fate forever bound to the ancient library that had claimed him as its own. There, he would continue to devour ancient secrets of the universe.

As the final echoes of Eren's humanity dissolved and his spirit merged with the vast expanse of the library's endless stacks, the silence of the library returned. Its secrets lay hidden within the walls, waiting for the next unsuspecting traveler to cross its threshold and meet their fate.

THE RUBY NECKLACE

In the historic town of Black Creek, where horses hooves clicked over cobblestone streets, gaslight lamps that lined walkways cast a warm glow, and Victorian mansions towered over bypassers, there stood a grand old house known as the Ashworth Manor. More than a century ago, it had been the home of Eleanor Ashworth, a wealthy heiress known for her kindness, generosity, philanthropy, and her prized possession—a stunning ruby necklace, said to be worth a king's ransom.

One fateful night, on the eve of her thirty-second birthday, Eleanor's life was brutally cut short. A group of unscrupulous men, driven by greed and cunning, observed as the banker responsible for her accounts carefully removed the necklace from the bank vault, preparing to deliver it for her birthday party the following day. Once the banker departed Ashworth Manor, they seized their chance and broke into her home. The men shot and killed any servant they came across as they made their way through the house and up to Eleanor's bedroom. Having heard the commotion downstairs, Eleanor locked herself in. However, the locks and door were no match for the men's determination. With a loud crack, they broke down the door and cornered her, demanding she hand over the ruby necklace. When she refused, they showed no mercy. Eleanor was murdered, her throat slashed in a manner so gruesome it left a vivid, bloody reminder of her beloved necklace.

The men were never caught as there were no witnesses left alive in the house to testify or make any identifications. Soon after, the house gained a sinister reputation. It was said that Eleanor's spirit remained in the house, seeking vengeance on those who wronged her. Anyone who bought the house and stayed there on the anniversary of her murder met a grisly end. Many neighbors, horrified by what had happened and determined not to

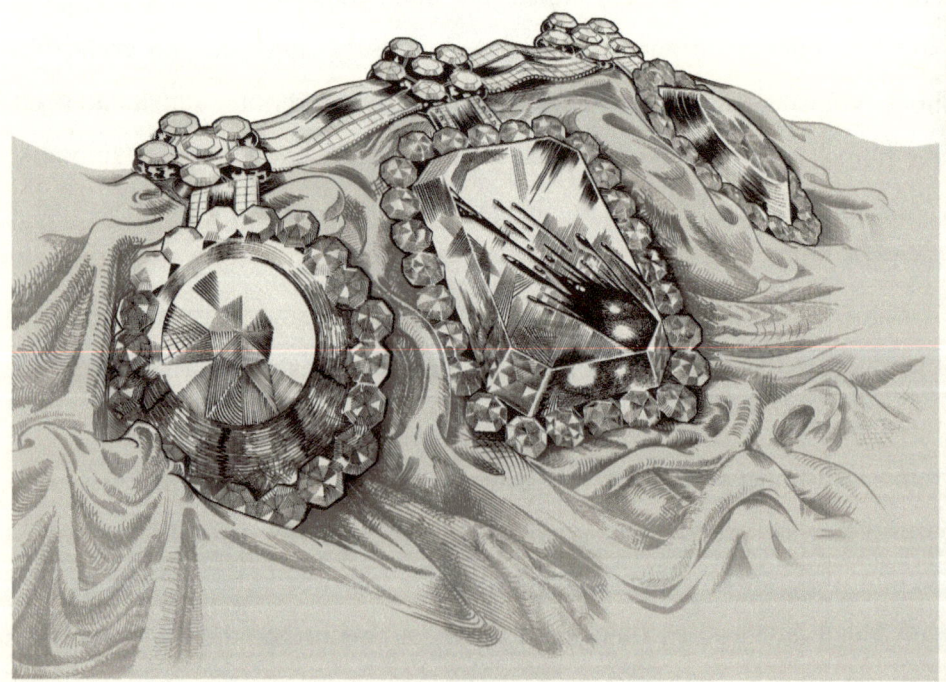

face a similar fate, left the area and sold their homes to anyone willing to take them. The legend of the "Ruby Necklace" curse grew, and the house stood boarded up and empty for years, shunned by the overly superstitious.

One autumn, a young couple named Lisa and Mark moved to Black Creek, seeking a fresh start away from the hustle and bustle of the big city.. Unfazed by the house's dark history and enticed by its low price, they bought Ashworth Manor. Despite the warnings from their new neighbors and the newspaper stories of grizzly murderers over the last century, they dismissed the tales as mere folklore and settled into their new home.

The house was beautiful, with grand rooms, ornate furniture left by previous owners, and a sense of faded elegance that the couple planned to restore. Lisa found herself drawn to the master bedroom, where a large portrait of Eleanor Ashworth still hung on the wall. Eleanor's eyes seemed to follow her. Perhaps a trick of the light, Lisa thought.

The weeks rolled by and the couple restored the house room by room. They found historic wallpaper to match that which was lost, refinished the floors, and had the exterior of the house painted. Nearly a year had gone by and, as the anniversary of Eleanor's murder approached, Lisa and Mark began to notice strange occurrences throughout the house. Footsteps could be heard in empty hallways, doors creaked open on their own, and the temperature in the master bedroom dropped to an icy chill each night.Some nights, it sounded as if someone had broken into the house, but when Mark checked the cameras, he found nothing. Lisa felt an increasing sense of dread, but Mark remained skeptical, insisting it was all in her imagination. "It's just an old house", Mark reminded her, "They all creak and moan and have poor insulation." Still, Lisa couldn't shake the feeling that something was off and that they should get as far away from the house as possible.

On the night of the anniversary, a violent storm raged outside. Lightning flashed, illuminating the eerie silhouette of the mansion. Lisa, unable to sleep, wandered through the darkened halls, her heart pounding with unease. She entered the master bedroom, staring at Eleanor's portrait. The eyes seemed to burn with an intensity she hadn't noticed before.

Suddenly, the room plunged into darkness, and a chilling wind swept through the house. Lisa heard a faint, whispering voice, growing louder and more insistent. She turned to leave but found the door slammed shut, trapping her inside. Panic seized her as the temperature plummeted further, her breath visible in the freezing air.

A ghostly figure materialized before her, the spectral form of Eleanor Ashworth. Her once-kind face twisted in anguish and fury. In her hand, she held the ruby necklace, dripping with blood. The whispering grew to a deafening roar, and Lisa's screams echoed through the house.

Mark, hearing his wife's cries, raced to the bedroom. He found the door locked, but with a desperate shove, he broke it open. Inside, he saw Lisa on the floor, her neck slashed in a grotesque mimicry of the ruby necklace, her lifeblood pooling around her.

The room was filled with a malevolent energy, the air thick with the presence of Eleanor's vengeful spirit. Mark, frozen in terror, watched as the ghostly figure turned to him, her eyes blazing with righteous fury. He tried to flee, but an unseen force held him in place.

The police arrived the next morning, responding to Mark's frantic 911 call before his fate was sealed. They found the couple dead, their necks slashed in the same horrific manner, as if adorned with a blood-red ruby necklace. The legend of Ashworth Manor and the vengeful spirit of Eleanor Ashworth was confirmed in the minds of locals.

Several years later the manor was demolished and highrise apartments went up in its place. However, each year, on the anniversary of her death, another victim would be claimed, ensuring that the tale of the Ruby Necklace lived on, a chilling legacy of a horrific murder. Today, the apartment stands empty and alone. Windows shattered by bricks thrown by unruly children, and the grounds overgrown. The darkened windows seemed to watch over the sidewalks, like eyes waiting patiently. Some people, while walking by the property, claim to see a woman dressed in Victorian clothing hiding in the shadows and peering down at them through one of the open windows. Then, suddenly, a glimmer of red from a necklace she wears catches their eye before she vanishes without a trace.

A few days ago, to the dismay of the neighbors, a sign was erected in front of the property that read,

Coming Soon:

Luxurious 1-3 Bedroom Condos.

THE LIGHTHOUSE

In the rugged coastline of Maine, where the Atlantic crashes against seaweed and moss covered cliffs, there stands a lighthouse steeped in sorrow and shadow. Perched atop a jagged promontory, its beacon once guided sailors safely through treacherous waters, but now it serves as a harbinger of doom.

Legend tells of a woman in white who haunts the lighthouse, her ghostly form drifting through the mist like a wraith. Her presence is most powerful during thunderstorms, when fierce winds hurl waves against the cliffs, shrouding the shore in sea mist. It is said she was the keeper's wife, her heart forever entwined with the sea by a boundless love. Her husband, a sailor of the vast ocean, shared a love as tempestuous as the storms that battered the coast.

But fate is a cruel mistress, and one stormy night, her beloved's ship was lost to the depths, swallowed whole by the hungry sea. When news of his

demise reached her ears, the keeper's wife was consumed by grief, her soul rent asunder by the crushing weight of her loss.

One night, she ascended to the lighthouse, clinging to the hope that she might see her beloved's ship returning home, despite the news of his demise. As hours slipped by, her hope waned until she heard the clock in the town square chime midnight. In a moment of despair, she climbed the spiral stairs of the lighthouse, her white dress billowing around her like a shroud, and flung herself from the dizzying heights, her anguished cries lost in the howling wind.

Since that fateful night, the lighthouse has been cursed, its halls haunted by the echoes of her sorrow and, at midnight, the very walls weep sea water. They say that anyone who hears her mournful wails is doomed to a fate worse than death— mere minutes to live before the specter of the woman in white claims them as her own.

And so it was that Emily, a young journalist with an unquenchable thirst for adventure and a mission to uncover any evidence that would prove the supernatural exists, found herself on the rocky coast of Maine researching alleged haunted properties. When she first heard whispers of the haunted lighthouse in a nearby village, and the tragic tale of the heartbroken widow who still wandered its spiral staircase and the lonely lantern room at the top, she felt an undeniable pull, as if the very winds were calling her to uncover its secrets. Ignoring the warnings of locals, Emily jumped into her car and made her way to the next village and, after a brief stop for directions and to fill up on gas, to the old lighthouse.

When she finally arrived, a storm began to brew over the Atlantic. She drove through the overgrown landscape until she couldn't drive any further.

Emily parked her car, grabbed her bag and continued on foot. After several minutes of walking, the trees parted to reveal the lighthouse towering on the horizon. Its exterior was deteriorating, with boards scattered around the ground where they had fallen off its side. As she reached the base of the lighthouse, the wind whipped around her, tearing at her clothes and hair. Her instincts told her to turn back, but Emily pressed on, her determination unyielding. She finally stood before the towering structure, its windows gazing out like hollow eyes.

With each step she took, the air grew heavier, as if weighted down by centuries of sorrow. And then, she heard it—the faintest whisper on the wind, a mournful cry that sent shivers down her spine. She pulled her cellphone from her pocket and began recording what she was hearing and seeing. With minimal effort, the door creaked open loudly, the sound echoing up through the entire tower.

Ignoring the voice of reason that screamed in her mind, Emily ascended the stairs, her footsteps echoing in the empty silence. And there, at the top of the lighthouse, she saw her—a woman in white standing outside the lantern room, her eyes empty and hollow, her ghostly form bathed in the pale light of the moon.

It was too late for Emily; she had already sealed her fate with her reckless pursuit. As the woman in white reached out to her with spectral hands, Emily's heart clenched with terror, realizing her mistake and feeling that her time was running out.

And so, as the storm raged on outside, Emily met her end within the haunted confines of the lighthouse, her screams lost in the howling wind. As the first light of dawn broke over the horizon, her lifeless body lay crumpled on the floor of the lantern room, a victim of the curse that had claimed so many before her.

For in the end, there is no escape from the woman in white and her eternal sorrow, only the cold embrace of death and the endless depths of the sea.

VANDERWYCK

Eldritch Hollow, long gone now, was an eerie, mist-shrouded town where the air echoed with whispers of ancient secrets and shadows seemed to harbor forgotten tales of the past. On the outskirts of the village, perched on a cliff overlooking the sea, stood the imposing mansion of the Vanderwyck family. The mansion, with its gothic spires and ivy-covered walls, bore witness to centuries of the family's dark legacy.

The Vanderwycks were no ordinary family; they were descendants of an arcane bloodline that traced its roots back to a time when magic intertwined with the very fabric of reality. The family had mastered the forbidden arts, unlocking powers that transcended the boundaries of mortal understanding. It was said that the Vanderwycks could traverse dimensions, manipulate the elements, communicate with otherworldly entities, and play with time so that they never die.

As the years passed, the townsfolk grew wary of the family and their supernatural abilities. The locals whispered tales of apparitions seen in the moonlit windows of the mansion, of spectral figures dancing in the overgrown gardens, and of shadows that moved of their own accord. Some of the elderly claim that members of the Vanderwyck family appear no older than 21, despite having known them for more than 80 years. But the true horror lay within the walls of the ancient estate.

The patriarch of the Vanderwyck family, Lord Archibald, was a domineering, ominous figure with gray eyes that held the weight of centuries. He could trap souls by casting them into mirrors and summon them at any time, bending them to his will. Every reflective surface in the mansion served as a portal to a realm of shadows and phantoms, through which the family could freely traverse. Each member possessed a distinct and extraordinary power within these realms.

The mansion itself seemed alive, responding to the commands of the family. Statues that adorned the grand hallways were not merely decorative; they were brought to life with a sinister animation, their cold stone eyes watching intruders with a malevolent gaze. Servants, long departed from the realm of the living, were reanimated to tend to the macabre needs of the family, which may have served them well, as no one in the village would dare take up employment at the manor.

The townsfolk lived in perpetual fear, afraid to cross paths with the Vanderwycks or to catch even a glimpse of the spectral manifestations that roamed the estate. Rumors spoke of disappearances—people who had dared to venture too close to the mansion, never to return. Eldritch Hollow became a place of dread, its streets deserted after nightfall as the town succumbed to the darkness that emanated from the mansion. The village

council banned mirrors fearing that the Vanderwycks could use them as portals for travel or spying. They decreed that all mirrors in the village be destroyed—smashed into pieces and cast into the sea. Only two villagers dared venture into the great estate to retrieve anything that might help the town rid themselves of the Vanderwycks. Out of the two, only one came back with an ancient book of black magic and mystical relics stolen from the family's vast library.

One fateful night, a brave group of villagers decided to rid themselves of the Vanderwyck family and put an end to the darkness that had long plagued Eldritch Hollow. Armed with the stolen ancient, magical relics and incantations passed down through the ages, they marched towards the foreboding mansion, their hearts pounding with a mix of determination and fear. Relics in hand and the ancient book of spells, they made their way to the mansion.

As they breached the gates, a cold wind whispered through the air, carrying with it the echoes of the family's dark laughter. The battle that unfolded within those haunted halls was a clash between the arcane and the mortal, a struggle that would determine the fate of Eldritch Hollow. A storm suddenly began to develop and swirl in the sky above the mansion as the family summoned the elements. Lightning flashed and, like hands, grabbed at the villagers, taking them out one-by-one. As one villager was lost, another would join in to push back against the Vanderwycks. As the villagers read from the book, each chanting in unison, a bright glow surrounded the ancient book of spells and, like a cannon, began to shoot out orbs that scattered throughout the manor, enabling members of the arcane family. Both sides fought violently and the villagers pushed on into the mansion, deeper and deeper.

Yet, as the final incantations echoed through the grand hallways, the mansion itself seemed to rebel against the intruders. Statues twisted and contorted, mirrors shattered, and the very walls groaned with a metallic rage. The Vanderwycks fought with a ferocity that transcended the mortal realm, unwilling to relinquish the power they had amassed over the centuries. As their powers dwindled, the villagers turned their own magic against them. The facade of youth dissolved, revealing the decrepit visages of age and malevolence beneath. Their once-grand attire now hung in tatters, rotting away like their fading essence. With screeches and groans that echoed through the night, they unleashed bursts of crimson energy from their eyes and gnarled hands, desperate to fend off the relentless onslaught of the villagers.

As the climax approached, the mansion convulsed and crumbled upon itself, its ethereal dimensions folding inward like a shredded page. The family, ensnared by the very arcane forces they had wielded, screamed futilely as they slowly dissolved into the gaping void that tore open in the earth below. In an instant, they were swallowed whole, and the void sealed shut, marking the Vanderwycks' inexorable descent into the abyss of Hades. Unified, the villagers watched as the mansion vanished abruptly, leaving behind only memories. The land beneath the mansion separated from the earth with a mighty quake and drifted into the sea, where it became an isolated island, cut off from the rest of the village.

With the darkness lifted, sunlight spilled over Eldritch Hollow, painting the village in warm hues of orange and yellow for the first time in years. The community, liberated from terror's grip, began to mend, though the enduring scars of the Vanderwyck legacy lingered in their collective consciousness.

To this day, locals avoid the scorched earth where the once-grand mansion stood, for they say that the Vanderwycks may have been banished, but the echoes of their supernatural reign still whisper in the shadows and can be heard across the waters, waiting for an opportune moment to return and cast their dark magic upon the unsuspecting world once more.

Labyrinth of the Witch

In the remote mining village of Eldershade, nestled at the edge of a dark and foreboding forest, a tale of a disappearing cottage had been passed down from father to son, mother to daughter, generation to generation. This eerie abode was said to manifest randomly every few years, and those who sought it did so in the hope of finding unimaginable riches. However, this quest was fraught with peril, for the cottage was home to a malevolent witch who ensnared those who lingered too long within her ever-changing labyrinth.

On a cold, mist-laden evening, a young and ambitious miner named Marcus, fairly new to town, decided he would find the hidden cottage. The villagers, wary and somber, warned him of the dangers and the many who searched adn were never seen again. But Marcus, with the arrogance of youth and a heart full of greed, dismissed their fears as mere folklore. He was confinced that the so-called "cottage" was nothing more than an

abandoned tunnel, a relic from miners long gone, concealing untold riches. The guardian, in his mind, was merely a clever trickster — miner who had spun a tale of terror to keep others from claiming the treasure for themselves.

As night fell, a peculiar stillness settled over the forest as Marcus came to the edge of the village. The moon hung low, casting an ethereal glow upon the forest's edge. For a moment Marcus looked back to the village, wondering if any of the stories might be true. Then, with a low chuckle, he shook his head and ventured into the woods, the path ahead illuminated by his flickering lantern. Hours seemed to stretch into eternity as he navigated the dense underbrush, his anticipation mounting with each step. He looked for any sign of an old track that might lead to an old tunnel.

Then, as if summoned by his very presence, a cottage appeared. It was a quaint, unassuming structure, its weathered facade belying the treacherous maze within. It seemed to materialize out of the mist. Heart pounding, Marcus approached the door, his thoughts consumed by visions of gold and jewels. He reached for the ornately cast doorknob, but before his fingers could grasp it, the knob twisted on its own. The door creaked open slowly, the hinges groaning as if in protest, echoing through the stillness. With a deep breath, he stepped inside, finding himself in a dimly lit entryway. Shadows clung to the corners, and the faint flicker of candlelight barely pierced the gloom..

The interior was a disorienting expanse, far larger than its modest exterior suggested. Endless corridors stretched before him, twisting and turning in bewildering patterns. The walls, adorned with faded tapestries, seemed to pulsate with a life of their own, shifting every few seconds to create new and confounding pathways.

Undeterred, Marcus shook his head and pressed on, his lantern casting eerie shadows that danced along the shifting walls. He encountered rooms filled with ancient relics, long-forgotten treasures, and strange artifacts that hinted at the cottage's dark history. His excitement grew with each discovery, but so did the unease that gnawed at the edges of his mind

As the hours wore on, Marcus's initial confidence gave way to a creeping dread. The corridors seemed to conspire against him, leading him in circles and deeper into the heart of the cottage. He could feel the presence of the witch, an unseen force that watched his every move with malevolent glee. In a grand hall lined with mirrors, Marcus caught a glimpse of something that made his blood run cold. Reflected in the glass was not his own weary visage, but the leering face of the witch. Her eyes, cold and merciless, bore into his soul, and a sinister smile curled her lips.

Panic seized him as the witch's laughter echoed through the twisting corridors. He turned and fled, but the walls shifted with alarming speed, the very structure of the cottage mocking his desperation. Marcus recalled the warning of a villager: anyone foolish enough to enter the witch's cottage had to find the exit before it vanished, or they would be trapped within its cursed confines, doomed to serve the witch for eternity.

In a final, frantic burst of speed, Marcus stumbled and fell into one of the tapestries hanging from the wall. To his astonishment, there was no wall behind it. Instead, he tumbled into a hidden chamber, its dim light glinting off piles of gold, jewels, and priceless artifacts scattered across the floor. For a fleeting moment, greed clouded his judgment, and he reached out to grasp a gleaming necklace. But the witch's voice, low and menacing, whispered in his ear, "Stay, and all this can be yours."

Terror jolted him back to his senses. He abandoned the treasure and raced through the maze, the corridors shifting faster and faster, the walls closing in. Just as the first light of dawn pierced the forest canopy, Marcus burst through the cottage door and tumbled onto the forest floor.

Behind him, the cottage slowly vanished, swallowed by the mist. He lay there, gasping for breath, the witch's laughter still ringing in his ears. He had escaped, but the memory of the maze and the witch's malevolent gaze would haunt him forever. As he prepared to flee, something on the ground caught his eye, glimmering in the dim light. He bent down and picked up a ring, its centerpiece a blood-red ruby set in solid gold—the most exquisite piece of jewelry he had ever seen.

Marcus returned to Eldershade, his lust for riches replaced by a profound respect for the legend. The villagers, upon seeing the haunted look in his eyes and the ruby ring clutched in his hand, understood that he had witnessed the terrifying truth of the disappearing cottage and its dark mistress. He was one of the fortunate few to have escaped its cursed grasp.

And so, the legend lived on, a chilling reminder of the perils that awaited those who sought fortune within the haunted forest. For the witch's cottage would reappear, luring the greedy and the foolish into its labyrinthine grasp, where they would face their doom or, by some miracle, emerge forever changed.

COME BACK TO ME, MY LOVE

Just outside the city, atop a large hill and nestled among dark woods, stood the old, imposing Blackthorn Manor. Unoccupied for decades, it was rumored to be haunted by a restless spirit that drove away anyone who dared to move in. After countless failed attempts to sell the property, realtors gave up, declaring it unsellable. Neighbors and those who knew the stories avoided the mansion and its grounds, yet they were eager to spread tales of its ghostly inhabitants and eerie occurrences. Around campfires and on stormy nights, they recounted the unsettling events that had transpired within its decaying walls years ago.

One stormy summer night, a group of curious and mischievous teenagers, obsessed with ghost stories and the thrill of the supernatural, decided to explore Blackthorn Manor. Determined to uncover the truth, they set out to discover whether the old mansion was truly haunted. Armed with flashlights and fueled by the jittery energy of gas station drinks, they biked to the outskirts of town where the streetlights ended and darkness took over. Circling the iron gates of the property, they found a bent section wide enough for them to squeeze through. Hiding their bikes behind overgrown shrubs, they pushed their way through the twisted iron. Before long, the imposing facade of Blackthorn Manor loomed before them. They quickly spotted a way in, slipping through a broken cellar window, unaware of the chilling presence that awaited them inside.

As they made their way through the maze of a cellar they finally came upon a rickety old staircase where they made their ascent into the grand manor. The door swung open and they found themselves in an enormous grand foyer shrouded in cobwebs that strung from floors to chandeliers. Wallpaper hung off the wall like decaying flesh and fell in ribbons on the floor. As they ventured deeper into the shadowy corridors, the air grew thick with an otherworldly energy. Disembodied whispers began to echo through the corridors and above them in the rafters of the great manor. Tendrils of cold air crept over their raindrop-splattered skin, sending shivers down their spines. Undeterred, the teenagers pressed on, fueled by a mix of fear and curiosity.

Finally, they came upon two mammoth doors covered in carvings of cherubs and mystical creatures that seemed to peer down at them through thin veils of spiderwebs. The doors made an awful groaning sound, like that of a beast, when pushed open. The teens stumbled through the entrance and found themselves in the grand salon. The walls were covered in spotted, dusty mirrors that reflected the grandeur of the room, making it seem twice as large. Mammoth crystal chandeliers hung from the ornate ceiling, their garlands broken and scattered across the floor. At the end of the grand salon sat an old, ornate piano covered in a dusty white sheet. Suddenly, out of the corner of their eyes, they noticed a green glowing orb floating around in the wall of mirrors. The orb seemed to move through the mirrors and into the grand salon where it hovered over the piano. Their flashlights flickered briefly before plunging into darkness.

Without warning, the sheet lifted, revealing spectral hands playing a haunting melody. The ghostly notes filled the air, resonating with a melancholic sadness that seemed to seep from the very walls.

As the teenagers stood frozen, a ghostly figure materialized at the piano - a woman in a tattered gown with hollow eyes. Her ethereal voice whispered a sorrowful tale of lost love and betrayal. "Come back to me, my love…" her voice echoed in ghostly tones. "Let us spend eternity together."

The room quivered with her lament, and the once-dead flowers on the tables around the salon bloomed for a fleeting moment. In the mirrors the teenagers caught glimpses of men and women in tuxedos and gowns, walking around the salon. A waltz could be heard in the distance. Suddenly, the room plunged into darkness as the woman at the piano rose from the bench. A revolver materialized on the piano top, which she seized, pressing the barrel to her temple and pulling the trigger. The sharp "BANG" of the gunshot reverberated through the salon, and lightning flashed in the mirrors, casting eerie reflections. The thunder clapped so loud that the mirrors shattered into millions of pieces and flew in all directions across the grand salon.

Terrified, the teenagers dropped their flashlights and fled from the manor, their screams piercing the night. The ghostly melody trailed behind them until they reached the gap in the gates. As they looked back, the front

doors slammed shut with a resounding bang, and a wailing cry echoed across the grounds, sending shivers down their spines. From that night on, the townsfolk claimed that on stormy evenings, the mournful strains of a piano could still be heard echoing through the desolate halls of the Manor. The final wail would be followed by the sharp crack of gunfire, and then… silence, once again.

The rumors and stories of Ravenscroft persisted. Eventually, the town had the property fenced in and locked away, allowing nature to take over. The old mansion remained a silent witness to the spectral serenade that lingered, forever etched into the haunted history of the town and the horrific tragedy that unfolded in the manor so many years ago. Today, in the fall when the leaves abandon the trees, one can still see the top floors of Blackthorn Manor. Her darkened windows looked down like haunting eyes… beckoning you to come inside.

The Mist of Darkmoor Lake

Deep in the dense, untamed wilderness of Darkmoor Lake, there stood an old, weathered cabin. Despite its picturesque location, the cabin had been for rent for many years, yet no one dared to stay there. Whispers of its dark past and tales of unspeakable horrors kept potential tenants at bay. It was said that the land the cabin stood on was cursed by natives centuries ago, and the mist that crept across the lake and into the woods was the manifestation of its sinister history.

One holiday weekend, the last weekend of summer, four friends—Alex, Sam, Jessica, and Lily—decided to visit somewhere new. They studied a map, searching for a place within a two-hour drive that caught their interest. Lily spotted a lake named Darkmoor just an hour away, a place none of them had heard of before. They searched surrounding rental sites and found a cabin listed at an astonishingly low price and, unaware of its grim reputation, eagerly booked it for a weekend getaway. Excited for a retreat in

nature, they packed their gear and set out for Darkmoor Lake.

To their surprise, the cabin was nestled deep in the woods, far from the other cabins and summer homes around the lake. They left the car in a public parking lot and, after an hour of trekking through the thick forest, they finally arrived at the far East edge of the lake. The sun was beginning to set, casting an eerie glow over the water. A thick mist began to rise from the lake, slowly creeping towards them. Undeterred, the friends continued, their excitement mingling with a growing sense of unease. Since it was getting late, they decided against exploring the area until morning.

The cabin loomed before them, a relic of the long forgotten past. Its wooden exterior was weathered and covered in moss, and the windows were cracked and filthy, giving it a haunted appearance. As they approached, the mist caught up with them, enveloping the house and its surroundings.

They entered the cabin, its interior filled with dust and cobwebs. The floorboards creaked under their weight, and the air was thick with the scent of decay.

Jessica sighed in disappointment. "Well... I guess we know why it was so cheap."

"Don't worry. We didn't come here for the cabin anyway. We came to explore the lake," Alex said optimistically.

They set up their sleeping bags in the main room, lighting a fire in the old stone fireplace to ward off the cold. As night fell, the mist outside grew thicker, pressing against the windows like a living entity. The four shared stories and laughter, ignoring the oppressive atmosphere. But as the hours passed, the mood grew somber. Strange noises echoed through the cabin— whispers, footsteps, and the faint sound of something scraping against the walls.

Jessica was the first to notice it. "Do you hear that?" she asked, her voice uneasy.

The others listened, their faces growing pale as the noises grew louder. The whispers seemed to come from all directions, and the scraping sound was now unmistakable. It was as if something was trying to claw its way inside.

Suddenly, the fire in the fireplace flickered and slowly died out, plunging the room into darkness. Panic set in, and they fumbled for their flashlights. In the dim beams, they saw movement in the corners of the room—shadows shifting and writhing as if alive.

"We need to get out of here," Alex said, his voice barely above a whisper.

They gathered their things quickly and made their way to the door, but it wouldn't budge. Alex and the others slammed their shoulders against the door with no luck. The mist outside had thickened, pressing against the cabin like a living, breathing creature. The windows, too, were impenetrable, covered by a film of ice despite the relative warmth of the season.

Trapped, the friends huddled together in the center of the room, their fear palpable. The whispers grew louder, forming words that chilled them to the bone.

"Staaaaay..."

The cabin seemed to come alive, the walls pulsating and the floorboards creaking ominously. Lily screamed as a hand, cold and clammy, emerged from the mist and grabbed her ankle, pulling her towards the shadows. The others tried to pull her back, but the force was too strong. She disappeared into the darkness, her screams abruptly cut off.

One by one, the friends were taken by the mist. Sam was dragged into the fireplace, his body contorting as he was pulled through the narrow chimney. Jessica was pulled into a dark corner, her flashlight dropping to the floor, illuminating her terrified face for a brief moment before she vanished.

Alex was the last one standing. He backed into a corner, clutching a rusted old poker he had found by the fireplace. The whispers grew louder, now a cacophony of voices demanding his surrender.

"Join us... forever..."

The mist closed in, and Alex swung the poker wildly, but it passed through the fog as if it were nothing. He felt cold hands grasping at him, pulling him down. His vision blurred, and he felt himself being drawn into the darkness.

The next morning, the cabin stood silent and empty, the mist receding as the sun rose. A group of hikers found the friends' abandoned campsite by the lake. They ventured into the woods, drawn by an inexplicable sense of dread. When they reached the cabin, they found it in ruins, with no sign of the friends.

The stories of the cabin at Darkmoor Lake spread far and wide, filled with chilling accounts of disappearances and deaths. The townsfolk, gripped by fear, warned outsiders to stay away, yet each year, curiosity lured new victims to the haunted site.

In a desperate attempt to end the horrors, a group of townsfolk from the surrounding area gathered one year to demolish the cabin and burn its ruins. They watched as the flames consumed the remnants, believing they had finally put an end to whatever evil resided there.

However, the following week, during a hike past the property, they were horrified to find the cabin standing as if it had never been torn down. Determined, they demolished it once more and set the remains ablaze. Yet, the very next day, the cabin reappeared, untouched and intact, defying their every effort to banish it.

The property still appears from time to time on a local rental site. No records of ownership exist, and no one knows who or what lists the property online. The headline simply reads:

For Rent:

A quaint, secluded cabin deep in the serene woods. Perfect for those seeking to escape the monotony of everyday life and immerse themselves in the untouched beauty of nature. Experience a truly unique getaway, far from the prying eyes of the outside world.

PHANTOM'S PREY

In the secluded, primitive village of Blackwood Hollow, nestled deep within a forest where ancient trees towered over the foggy landscape, an ominous legend persisted. During each winter solstice, a phantom roamed the sleepy town, a specter of death and deceit.

The villagers, bound by fear and tradition, knew better than to venture out during this darkest night. Windows were shuttered, doors bolted, and fires stoked high to ward off the chilling presence that prowled their streets. Yet, despite their precautions, each solstice claimed a victim, leaving behind a tale of terror and sorrow.

On the eve of the winter solstice, the village seemed to hold its breath. Snow blanketed the ground, muffling sounds and lending an eerie stillness. In one home, a young woman named Eliza clung to her infant son, her heart pounding with the dread that filled the air.

"Stay inside, my love," her husband, Thomas, had whispered that morning before he ventured into the woods to gather extra firewood. He had yet to return, and with the solstice night upon them, Eliza's anxiety grew.

As the night deepened, a knock echoed through the heavy silence. Eliza's heart leapt into her throat. "Thomas?" she called out, hope mingling with fear. She approached the door cautiously, peering through the small window.

There stood her husband, snow-dusted and weary, his familiar smile easing her fears. She unlatched the door, and he stepped inside, embracing her and their child. "I made it back just in time," he murmured, his voice comforting.

Relief washed over Eliza, but a shadow of doubt lingered. The legend of the phantom gnawed at her mind. She glanced at Thomas, noticing the coldness of his skin, the slight unnatural stiffness in his movements. But she shook off her unease, attributing it to her frayed nerves.

As the night wore on, Thomas sat by the fire, his eyes flickering with an intensity that unsettled Eliza. She watched him closely, her instincts screaming that something was amiss. The baby stirred in her arms, and Thomas's gaze snapped to them with a predatory glint. Eliza's blood ran cold. She knew then, with a heart-wrenching certainty, that this was not her husband. The phantom had found its way into her home.

With a burst of desperate courage, Eliza clutched her child and ran for the back door. The creature that wore Thomas's face lunged after her, its fingers elongating into ghastly claws. She stumbled into the snow, the cold biting at her skin, but she pressed on, driven by a primal need to protect her child.

The villagers, hearing her cries, peeked from their windows, horror

etching their faces as they saw the phantom in pursuit. They dared not venture out, paralyzed by their own terror.

Eliza's strength waned as she reached the edge of the village. She collapsed, shielding her baby with her body. The phantom loomed over her, its true form flickering through the facade of her husband's face.

"Please," she whispered, her voice trembling, "spare my child."

The phantom paused, a flicker of humanity crossing its spectral features. But the hunger for life was too great. It reached down, ready to drain her life force, when the first light of dawn broke over the horizon.

The solstice night ended, and with it, the phantom's time in the mortal realm. It recoiled with a hiss, the illusion of Thomas disintegrating into a swirl of shadows. The wraith retreated into the forest, leaving behind the withered husk of its latest victim.

The villagers found Eliza the next morning, cradling her child, her body cold and lifeless. They buried her with solemn reverence, another soul claimed by the curse of Blackwood Hollow.

The legend lived on, a grim reminder of the price of crossing paths with the phantom during the winter solstice. And each year, as the days grew shorter and the solstice approached, the village would once again lock their doors and wait in fearful silence, hoping to survive another night of terror.

THE WATCHER IN THE ATTIC

In the small, isolated town of Cold River, there stood an old, decrepit home known as the Winslow House. Everyone avoided the very street it sat on and the house had been abandoned for decades, its windows boarded up and its doors chained shut. But for Jason and Emily, a young couple looking for an affordable place to start their new life, the Winslow House seemed like a hidden gem, despite its eerie reputation.

They purchased the house at a remarkably low price, dismissing the townspeople's warnings as mere superstition. The couple moved in, excited to restore the old house and turn it into their dream home. They spent their days cleaning, restoring, and renovating, slowly bringing life back to the dusty, cobweb-filled rooms. During the days they dreamt about the children they'd raise in the house and the parties they'd host. But as night fell, the atmosphere grew heavy, and an unsettling presence seemed to linger in the shadows.

One stormy night, while Jason was away on a business trip, Emily sat alone in the living room, the flickering fireplace casting shadows on the walls as she read a book of poetry. She heard a faint, rhythmic creaking sound coming from above. At first, she dismissed it as the house settling in the wind, but the noise persisted, growing louder and more deliberate. It seemed to come from the attic.

Worrying that an animal had somehow gotten into the house, Emily grabbed a flashlight and made her way up the narrow, creaky staircase leading to the attic. The door at the top was slightly ajar, and a cold draft seeped through the gap. She hesitated, her heart pounding, but curiosity compelled her to push the door open, hoping a critter didn't jump out at her.

The attic was filled with old furniture, dusty trunks, and forgotten photos. As she scanned the room with her flashlight, the beam caught something that made her blood run cold. In the far corner, a pair of eyes reflected the light, staring back at her. They were unnaturally large, gleaming with a malevolent intelligence.

Emily gasped and stumbled backward, dropping the flashlight. The room plunged into darkness, and she could hear the sound of something moving swiftly towards her. She scrambled to her feet and ran down the stairs, slamming the attic door behind her. She bolted to the bedroom, locking the door and hiding under the covers, her heart racing with terror.

The next morning, Jason returned to find Emily pale and trembling, her eyes wide with fear. She recounted her harrowing experience, but he remained skeptical, attributing it to her imagination and the stress of being alone in the old house.

Determined to prove her fears unfounded, Jason decided to investigate the attic himself. He grabbed a baseball bat from a closet and a flashlight and made his way up the stairs. The attic door was still shut, and he steeled himself before opening it.

The attic appeared empty, just as Emily had described, but there was an unnerving stillness in the air. Emily's flashlight was on the floor, its bulb and glass cover shattered all over the floor. As he explored the room, he noticed something odd: a small, hidden door behind an old wardrobe. It was barely noticeable, blending seamlessly with the wall. Jason forced it open, revealing a narrow passage that led to a hidden room.

Inside the room, he found a disturbing scene. The walls were covered in strange, ancient symbols, and in the center of the room was a crude altar made of old, rotting wood. Scattered around the altar were yellowed pages filled with cryptic writing and drawings of grotesque, otherworldly creatures.

As he examined the room, a cold chill ran down his spine, and he felt an oppressive presence watching him. Suddenly, the door slammed shut, and the room was plunged into darkness. Jason's flashlight flickered and died, leaving him in total blackness.

He heard the same creaking sound Emily had described, now louder and more menacing. Panicked, he fumbled for the door, but it wouldn't budge. The creaking grew closer, and he felt something brush against his arm. He swung the baseball bat wildly, but it connected with nothing.

In the darkness, a whispering voice filled the room, speaking in a language he couldn't understand. The air grew colder, and Jason felt an icy hand grip his shoulder. He screamed, the sound echoing through the house, and then there was silence.

Emily, waiting anxiously downstairs, heard the scream and ran to the attic. She found the door shut tight and no sign of Jason. Desperate, she called the police, but when they arrived, they found no trace of him. The hidden room was gone, the passage sealed as if it had never existed.

The locals shook their heads, their fears confirmed. The Winslow House had claimed another victim. Emily, heartbroken and terrified, left Cold River, never to return.

The house stood silent and abandoned once more, but the stories about the Watcher in the Attic continued, and whatever it was that took Jason was forever waiting for its next victim.

CURSE OF THE MUSIC BOX

In the quaint, picturesque town of Willow Creek, nestled among rolling hills and serene landscapes, there existed an old antique shop known as Abigail's Curiosities. The shop was filled with relics from bygone eras, each with its own history and mystery. Among the countless trinkets, one item stood out—a beautifully ornate music box, adorned with intricate carvings and inlaid with mother-of-pearl. It was said to be the last remaining possession of a once-renowned ballerina named Isabella.

The music box had a sinister reputation. It was rumored that anyone who played its haunting melody would be cursed, condemned to a fate worse than death. Despite the warnings, the allure of the music box was irresistible, and it remained a coveted piece in Abigail's collection.

One autumn afternoon, a young woman named Clara, new to the town and a lover of all things antique, wandered into the shop. She was immediately drawn to the music box. Its beauty and craftsmanship captivated her, and

despite the shopkeeper's grave warnings, Clara purchased it, dismissing the tales as mere superstition.

That night, in the comfort of her cozy cottage, Clara placed the music box on her bedside table. She hesitated briefly, recalling Abigail's warning, but curiosity got the better of her. She turned the key and opened the lid. A delicate, melancholic tune began to play, and a tiny ballerina twirled gracefully to the haunting melody.

As the music filled the room, Clara felt a chill run down her spine. The shadows in the corners seemed to deepen, and the air grew heavy with an unexplainable dread. She quickly closed the lid, but the eerie feeling lingered. Shaking off her unease, Clara went to bed, the music box still sitting ominously on her table.

In the dead of night, Clara was awakened by the faint sound of the music box playing on its own. The soft, haunting melody filled the room, and she felt an overwhelming sense of dread. She tried to move, but her body was paralyzed, pinned to the bed by an unseen force. The ballerina inside the music box began to spin faster, her delicate features twisting into a sinister grin.

Clara's eyes darted around the room, and she saw shadowy figures emerging from the corners, their forms shifting and writhing. They surrounded her bed, their hollow eyes fixed on her. The music grew louder, more frantic, and the figures began to whisper in a language she couldn't understand. Their voices were cold and filled with malice.

The ballerina's eyes glowed with an eerie light, and Clara felt herself being pulled into the music box. Her surroundings blurred, and she found herself standing in a vast, dark void, the only sound the relentless, haunting melody. The shadowy figures closed in, their whispers growing louder, filling her mind with despair and fear.

Clara tried to scream, but no sound escaped her lips. She felt her body being torn apart, her soul consumed by the darkness. The last thing she saw was the ballerina, now towering over her, its grin widening as it devoured her essence.

The next morning, Abigail's Curiosities was once again shrouded in an air of foreboding. The shopkeeper noticed that the music box had been returned, sitting innocently on the shelf, its lid slightly ajar. Inside, the ballerina twirled slowly, and a faint whisper echoed from within, "Join us..."

Clara was never seen again. Her name was added to the long list of those claimed by the cursed music box. Abigail knew better than to dispose of the relic, for its curse was bound to the shop, ensuring its malevolent presence would continue to lure and trap the curious and the foolish.

And so, the music box remained, a beautiful and deadly trap, waiting for another to succumb to its haunting melody. The shop's door would creak open, the bell would jingle, and another soul would be drawn to the mesmerizing tune, unaware of the dark fate that awaited them.

Carousel of Evil

Hidden deep within the labyrinthine corridors of an old, decrepit warehouse on the outskirts of a forgotten town lay an old carousel. It was covered in dust and shrouded in darkness, concealed within a vault locked tight with chains and padlocks. The carousel was a relic of a time in the town's history that had caused unspeakable horrors and was buried away to protect the children from its wickedness.

Decades ago, the carousel first arrived in the town as part of a traveling carnival. The town's children, drawn by its brightly colored lights and whimsical music, flocked to ride the beautifully carved horses and chariots. But as the carnival's festivities drew to a close, the town began to notice strange occurrences. Children who rode the carousel would vanish, their laughter echoing through the night but never returning home. Those who went looking for them found only empty seats, still warm from where the children had sat.

As the disappearances mounted, the town descended into panic. The carnival was ordered to leave by the city council, but the carousel was left behind, abandoned and rotting in the town square. Desperate to rid themselves of its curse, the townspeople dismantled the carousel and locked it away in a warehouse just outside of town, hoping to bury the terror it brought with it. But the carousel was not so easily forgotten.

Years passed, and the warehouse fell into disrepair. Vines crept over its walls, and rust consumed its metal frame. It became a place avoided by all, a tomb for the forgotten horrors of the past. The town's memory of the cursed carousel faded, becoming little more than a ghost story told by older generations around campfires and on Halloween night.

One day, at an auction, the warehouse came up for sale to cover many years of back taxes. Four out-of-towners attended the auction, unaware of the town's dark history and solely interested in a financially beneficial opportunity. Jake, Emily, Tom, and Lisa were antique dealers always on the lookout for hidden treasures. They had heard rumors about the old warehouse, a place filled with forgotten antiques and artifacts, and decided to purchase it, hoping to find something valuable among its dusty contents.

One fateful day, after the sale went through, they pried open the rusty door of the warehouse.For the first time in decades, light poured into the building and the air stirred up dust and cobwebs. As the four ventured deeper into the darkness, their footsteps echoed ominously against the cold, stone floor. They pulled out their cellphones to light their path. As they progressed, the air grew colder, and an unsettling silence enveloped them, broken only by the distant creak of metal and the occasional drip of water from the leaking ceiling.

"Look at all this old stuff!" Tom exclaimed, shining his flashlight on a stack of dusty crates filled with antique furniture and trinkets.

Emily nodded, her eyes scanning the room for anything particularly valuable. "We might actually hit the jackpot this time."

As they moved further into the warehouse, something caught Jake's eye. "Guys, over here!" he called, his voice reverberating through the cavernous space.

They followed him to a large, vault-like door, covered in chains and padlocks. Jake and Emily made their way back to their truck and returned with blow torches and tools. With a mix of excitement and curiosity, they set to work on the locks, their determination growing with each click of their tools. After what felt like an eternity, the last padlock fell away, and the door creaked open to reveal a hidden room.

Inside, illuminated by their phone flashlights, stood a grand carousel. Despite the passage of time, it was eerily intact, its horses frozen mid-gallop, their once vibrant paint now chipped and faded. The teams' eyes widened with greed and awe.

"This must be worth a fortune!" Lisa whispered, her voice tinged with excitement.

Driven by the prospect of a large payday, they approached the carousel. Jake reached out to touch one of the horses, and as his fingers brushed against the cold, wooden surface, a shiver ran down his spine. Suddenly, as if just a whisper, the carousel's music began to play, a haunting melody that seemed to emanate from the shadows themselves.

"Did you do that?" Lisa asked, her voice trembling.

Jake shook his head, stepping back as the carousel slowly began to turn on its own with a low, metallic creek. The horses moved up and down, their once graceful motions now grotesque and jarring. The air in the room grew thick with an unnatural fog that crawled out from under the carousels base, and the temperature plummeted.

"Let's get the hell outta here," Emily urged, but as they moved to leave, the warehouse door slammed shut with a deafening bang. Frantically, they tried their cell phones, only to find them mysteriously dead. Panic gripped them as the reality of being trapped sank in. Meanwhile, the carousel's music grew louder and more distorted, while thick fog enveloped them, making it difficult to see anything clearly.

From the mist, ghostly figures emerged—children with hollow eyes and skeletal hands, their mouths twisted in silent screams. They reached out to the four, their icy fingers grasping at their clothes and skin. They tried to fight them off, crying out for help, but their movements were sluggish, their strength sapped by the cold and fear.

The carousel continued to spin, its speed increasing with each rotation. The children pulled them toward the carousel as they kicked and screamed in vain, forcing them onto the horses. As the four sat on the cursed seats, their bodies froze, their eyes glazed over with the same hollow emptiness that plagued the lost children.

The carousel spun faster and faster, the music crescendoing to a fever pitch. Emily's mouth opened in a silent scream, engulfed by the cacophony, their forms ethereal and ghost-like, ensnared in an unending cycle of torment. Round and round the carousel whirled, until abruptly, the children and antique dealers vanished into thin air. The carousel lights flickered and the ride jerked to a stop. Darkness cloaked the carousel once more. After a fleeting moment, the cell phones they had dropped flickered back to life as the malevolent presence receded. The warehouse descended into silence once more, the carousel now motionless, its horses now ridden by new, hollow-eyed specters.

The curse of the carousel was true, and its hunger was insatiable. The townspeople, sensing the awakening of the old terror, sealed the warehouse tighter than before, but the story of the carousel and those lost would become another dark chapter in the town's history—a warning to all who dared to seek the thrill of the unknown.

Hidden in the vaults of the old warehouse, the carousel waits, its music silent for now, but the curse ever watchful, ready to claim new souls that disturbs its haunted slumber.

FROM THE AUTHOR
A PERSONAL GHOST STORY

A few years ago, my acting career in New York City had hit a wall, leaving me restless and frustrated. By summer, I'd resolved to leave the city, though I hadn't yet decided where to go.

A close friend of mine, who had recently uprooted her life and moved to Ohio, invited me to stay with her and her fiancé while I figured out where I wanted to go next. What was meant to be a temporary arrangement turned into a year-long stay, during which I settled into a full-time job and found myself surprisingly content with the slower pace of life in the Midwest.

My parents visited a few times and, charmed by the area, decided to sell their house and make the move to Ohio to be closer to me. They scoured listings, toured dozens of homes, but nothing seemed to fit. That's when my sister, who had been helping with online searches, sent us a link to a listing for a grand, old house in a historic district not far from the heart of the city. The photos were breathtaking, yet they didn't begin to do justice to the reality of the place. When we finally saw the house in person, it felt like stepping back in time.

The house was built with quarter-sawn oak throughout—door moldings, baseboards, floorboards, carved fireplace facades, built-in cabinets, and bookcases in the library, as well as china cabinets in the dining room. At the back of the foyer, an elegant, winding staircase led to the second-floor bedrooms and study. The second floor also included a maids' wing, with a good-sized room, a small hallway, and a servants' staircase that led down to the kitchen below.

With around 4,000 square feet of space, the house still had much of its original character: the woodwork, the old knob-and-tube electrical system, and even a garage—an unusual feature for a home built in 1904. Very little had been updated or altered over the years. It was exactly what my parents had been hoping for.

After weeks of bank visits and wading through piles of paperwork, the house was finally theirs. To celebrate, they got a German Shepherd puppy to keep them company in the large, now quiet house. Not long after settling in, my mother, feeling the weight of being over 16 hours away from the rest of the family, asked if I'd move in with them. At first, I was hesitant. My mother and I were so alike that we often clashed, and I wasn't sure how living together again would work. But I agreed, thinking it would help them settle in and give me some time before finding a place of my own.

A few weeks later, I was deep asleep in my room when a loud thud jolted me awake. I sat up, my eyes straining to adjust to the dark. When the thud came again, I got out of bed, moved quietly across the room, and slowly opened the door. I peered into the hall, where I saw the door to my parents' room ajar. My father's head poked out, followed closely by my mother. In a whisper, he asked, "Chad, was that you?"

I shook my head and glanced down the hall. All the bedroom doors were closed. Then it came again—a muffled thud, followed by the unmistakable sound of someone running up and down a flight of stairs. My father's gaze shifted to the door leading to the maids' wing. He whispered, "It's coming from there."

Without hesitation, he turned back to his room. I heard him murmur to my mother, "Stay in here and lock the door." Moments later, he emerged into the hallway, holding a handgun. His voice was calm but firm. "You head downstairs to the kitchen and come up the other way."

My pulse quickened as I darted downstairs, through the foyer, past the dining room, and into the kitchen. The sounds of hurried footsteps echoed from behind the door concealing the staircase to the maids' wing. My hands fumbled under the sink until they found a hammer. Gripping it tightly, I approached the door. The moment I turned the handle and pulled it open, the noises stopped.

"Dad!" I called up the stairs. The lights flickered on, and he appeared at the top, peering around the corner. Both of us stood there, baffled. Together, we checked every door in the house, ensuring they were locked. They all were.

The next day, my parents had every lock in the house changed. We couldn't shake the fear that it might have been a former occupant or a contractor from the bank—someone with a key, assuming the house would be empty.

A week later, we installed security cameras around the house, and every lock was replaced. That evening, the three of us were in the library, unwinding. My mother was immersed in a book, my father was focused on a game on his laptop, and I was scrolling through Instagram.

Out of nowhere, a loud crash echoed from the kitchen. We all jumped to our feet, assuming the weight of my mother's extensive china and crystal collection had finally caused the cupboards to give way. Rushing to the swinging door, we braced for chaos—but the kitchen was untouched. No broken glass, no fallen plates, nothing.

Perplexed, we opened every cupboard, drawer, and cabinet. When that revealed nothing, we headed to the basement, checking if any boxes had toppled over. Still, everything was in its place.

Later that afternoon, as we relaxed on the front porch, enjoying the warmer weather, we struck up a conversation with our next-door neighbors. Their house was just 20 feet from our kitchen windows. Casually, we asked if they had heard a crash or dropped something earlier. Their answer was a firm no.

The next night, I woke to the sound of knocking. It seemed to be coming from outside my window, which struck me as strange—there were no trees close enough to brush against the house.

I closed my eyes, trying to convince myself it was nothing, but then it came again. This time, the sound was downstairs. Knock… knock… knock. The pauses between each knock were unnervingly precise, sending a chill down my spine.

Grabbing my cellphone from the bedside table, I opened the security app to check the cameras at the front and back doors. Both feeds showed nothing but the empty night. Then, once more: knock… knock… knock.

Tossing off the covers, I stepped into the hallway, heart pounding. I scanned the area, checking for light under the doors of the bedrooms and the study. Everything was dark. I moved cautiously, opening each door quietly so as not to disturb my parents. I switched on the lights, making sure all the windows were securely shut.

Finally, I turned to the door leading to the third floor, a space we used mostly for storage. My footsteps echoed faintly as I climbed the stairs, the air cooler and heavier up there. I scanned the room, peering into every shadowy corner. Nothing.

Relieved but still uneasy, I returned to my room. Eventually, I fell into a restless sleep.

The next morning, around 5 a.m., I got dressed and headed downstairs to make breakfast. As I descended the main staircase, the faint sound of glasses clinking reached my ears, as though someone was carefully gathering dishes.

At the base of the stairs, the foyer stretched out before me. Built into the wall was a large, full-length mirror, framed in ornate oak columns and decorative moldings. To the left of the mirror were pocket doors leading to the drawing room; to the right, identical doors opened to the library. Directly across from the stairs, the dining room stood opposite the drawing room.

As I stepped off the staircase, something caught my eye—a flicker of movement in the mirror. I hesitated. From a certain spot in the foyer, the mirror's reflection gave a clear view into the dining room. Slowly, I moved to that spot, my pulse quickening. When I glanced into the mirror, I froze.

A woman was in the dining room. She moved gracefully, almost floating, toward the far end where the swinging door led into the kitchen. Her presence was unsettling, but I couldn't look away. The air around me felt heavy, and the faint clinking sound I'd heard moments earlier seemed to linger in the silence.

(This real-life encounter became the subject of the poem, "The Lady In The Mirror")

Naturally, I assumed it was my mother—there were no other women in the house. "Mother, what are you doing?" I called out. No answer. Frowning, I walked through the foyer and turned into the dining room. The swinging door to the kitchen was gently moving back and forth, creaking softly with each sway.

Annoyed, I pushed through into the kitchen, half-expecting my mother to jump out and laugh at her joke. "Mom?" I called, my voice sharp with irritation. No one was there. The kitchen was empty, the early morning light just beginning to filter through the windows. Determined to prove my suspicion, I yanked open the door to the servants' stairwell, convinced she was hiding there. Nothing. I checked the other doors, pulling on each one, but they were all locked—locked in a way that required a key to open.

As I stood there, gripping the edge of the counter, a chill swept over me. Every hair on my body stood on end as I replayed the moment in the mirror. My mother wasn't an early riser, and even if she was, she wasn't petite. The figure I'd seen had a tiny waist and a pronounced, almost exaggerated backside. It wore a long, flowing gown or nightdress—something my mother would never wear. And just before it disappeared from the mirror's edge, it had turned its head toward me.

There were no details on the face, but I knew it was looking at me. The realization sent a jolt of fear through me, and without thinking, I bolted back through the house and up the stairs to my parents' bedroom. I knocked once before flinging the door open.

Both my parents shot up in bed, startled and clearly disoriented. They had been fast asleep. Still, I demanded, "Were you just downstairs trying to scare me?" My voice was loud and trembling, my rational mind grasping for an explanation—any explanation that made sense. Deep down, I knew it wasn't possible. My mother couldn't have raced up the stairs without me hearing, and there was no way she could lock the doors behind her.

You see, I've always loved ghost stories and Halloween. But I've never believed in hauntings—not until we moved into this house.

The house had been built in a wealthy neighborhood at the turn of the century, surrounded by homes that were now historic landmarks. Hoping to uncover the history of our house, I visited the local records office to find out who had lived there and what had happened to them. Unfortunately, I learned that a devastating flood in 1913 had destroyed many of the area's records and claimed countless lives.

Just as I was about to give up, I was introduced to the president of a neighboring historic district. We became fast friends, and one day, while browsing through his collection of antique and vintage books, I stumbled across something extraordinary—a telephone directory from 1920. Though it was published 16 years after our house was built, I hoped it might still hold a clue about its past.

Flipping through the fragile pages, I found our street and carefully scanned the addresses, working my way down the numbers. Finally, I found it—our house. Listed under our address were three women with the same last name. Perhaps a mother and her daughters, or maybe three spinsters?

My curiosity was piqued.

But then I saw something else, something that sent chills racing up and down my spine. Beneath the women's names, written plainly in the same faded ink, was another line: "and maid."

It hit me all at once. The strange events—the knocking, the fleeting figure in the dining room mirror, the sounds of dishes clinking—seemed to revolve around the dining room, kitchen, and maids' wing. The pieces were falling into place, and the realization filled me with both fascination and unease.

A few weeks passed, and the knocking became sporadic. Strange sounds and footsteps occasionally echoed from the maids' wing and stairwell, but we did our best to ignore them. Over time, the noises seemed to fade altogether, and the house grew quiet once more.

Nearly a year later, my oldest sister announced her divorce. She moved to Ohio to stay with us for a while, bringing her three children along. The house, once settled, felt alive again—not just with their presence, but with something else. It wasn't long before the haunting resumed.

My niece chose the maids' room as her bedroom, drawn perhaps by its cozy isolation. Soon after, the knocking returned, accompanied by the familiar sounds of running footsteps in the stairwell. Late one night, around midnight, my sister burst into my room and shook me awake.

"Why are you trying to scare her?" she demanded, her tone sharp with anger. Groggy and confused, I blinked at her in the dim light, trying to process what she was saying. "What are you talking about?" I finally asked, my voice hoarse with sleep.

"You were banging on her door and running up and down the stairs!"

she snapped.

I stared at her, dumbfounded. "I've been asleep," I said, glancing at the clock. I had work early the next morning and couldn't fathom why she thought I'd do such a thing. Her expression shifted from anger to unease as she realized I was telling the truth.

Something—or someone—had returned, and this time, it didn't seem content to stay quiet.

When I pressed her for details, my sister explained that my niece had woken up to the sound of loud, aggressive knocking on her bedroom door. She'd opened it, only to find no one there. Moments later, the knocking started again. This time, when she opened the door, her shoes—which had been haphazardly scattered around the maids' hallway earlier—were perfectly aligned in a neat row, directly in front of the door.

I assured my sister that I hadn't done anything of the sort, and after some tense words, I went back to bed. But the strange occurrences didn't stop. Over the following months, cold spots began to appear at random around the maids' room, chilling the air even on the warmest days. Our German Shepherd, usually fearless, would growl low and menacingly at the door to the maids' wing. When we opened it, she would rush inside, frantically sniffing and searching the hall and room. Finding nothing, she'd settle at our feet, her ears back, letting out soft, anxious whimpers.

The tension in the house grew palpable, and before long, my sister had had enough. As soon as her divorce was finalized, she packed up her children and left. The maids' wing was abandoned after that, the door left closed and the lights off.

And just like that, the activity stopped again. The house fell silent, as if whatever had stirred had gone dormant—or left entirely.

A few years later, during the pandemic, all three of us fell seriously ill. After a long, difficult month, my mother passed away on Christmas Eve. Breaking the news to my father was one of the hardest things I've ever had to do. His health began to decline soon after, and just three weeks later, he passed away as well.

The house fell to me, and now I live here alone with our loyal German Shepherd, Gretchen. It's a big, quiet place without them, and though the memories are everywhere, the silence feels heavier than it ever did before.

A few weeks ago, the day after Thanksgiving, I was sitting in the library, trying to relax with a book. Gretchen lay on the rug by the fire, her head resting on her paws. Out of nowhere, she sprang up, her ears alert, and growled low at the window across the room. I froze, then turned to see what had caught her attention.

At that moment, I heard it: knock… knock… knock. The sound was muffled but unmistakable. My heart quickened as I reached for my phone and pulled up the security cameras. The feeds showed nothing unusual. Then it came again: knock… knock… knock.

I got up and began moving through the house, searching for the source. But each time I left the library, the knocking stopped. It was as if the sound refused to exist outside that room. Finally, unsettled and exhausted, I gave up and made my way upstairs to bed.

Normally, I leave my bedroom door open so Gretchen can come and go as she pleases. But that night, I couldn't shake the feeling of being watched. I locked the door, keeping her inside with me, and didn't leave until morning.

C.M. Wyckoff

Instagram: @cmwyckoff

www.sixteen37.com

www.ingramcontent.com/pod-product-compliance
Lightning Source LLC
Chambersburg PA
CBHW020231120726
47903CB00008B/2627